THE
BIG SIGH

by
Myr Skipper

DORRANCE PUBLISHING CO., INC
PITTSBURGH, PENNSYLVANIA 15222

DEDICATION

To all the children
who have me running with them
in meadows of dreams
where peace and love bloom
in all the colors of light
and our joyous sounds
reverberate throughout the Earth.

— Myr Skipper

Once on a beach there was a sigh. It was a big sigh, bigger than that of an old tree in the wind. It was bigger than an adult's sigh after a long day of hard work and bigger than a child's sigh when it is time for bed.

No one knew where the sigh came from as they heard it. Some people didn't hear the sigh as they talked, laughed, and threw their drink cans on the sand. They didn't notice anything but their drinks and each other, not even the pearly shells at their feet or the shore birds who lived there.

T hose who went to the beach and heard it knew it was there, though they didn't know its source. There were older people with gray hair who knew it had not always been there. They remembered walking and stopping to look at shells and shiny green seaweed brought in by the tide. Then, everything on the beach had belonged there, had fit together with the sea and the sky. It was all beautiful to their eyes and ears. It felt good to be there. Then one day they saw a can lying near the shells and a plastic bag tangled with the seaweed. It made them sad and angry, but they didn't do anything about it. They stepped over it as they walked and talked about it. Then they heard the sigh. Every season from then on there was more garbage on the beach and the sigh got bigger.

Younger people heard the sigh as well, knew it was there. Those who walked and ran and sometimes picked up shells as they enjoyed the sun and sea breeze felt happy until they saw the ugly garbage. They felt sad and angry as they kicked it aside and then they heard the sigh.

C hildren heard the sigh also, knew it was there. They loved to play on the beach, to build with the sand. They loved running into the waves and feeling the power of the water on their legs. They loved flying kites and feeling the wind in their faces. With excitement, they watched gulls rush for food as the tide went out. They put shells in their pockets and wrote their names in the sand with a finger. When the children who saw the dead bird strangled by a plastic container heard the sigh they became quiet and sad, but they didn't know why.

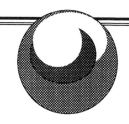

One day, a man and woman went to this beach for the first time. As they stood before descending the bank to the beach, they saw the deep blue water rising in waves and falling in white foam. They saw older people and younger people walking and children playing beneath a blue sky with puffy white clouds. The sound of the waves was like wonderful music. The sun felt warm and the air smelled like something good to eat. They looked up at a sudden sound and saw wings of white gliding through the blue. They looked at each other, smiled, grabbed hands and ran laughing down the bank. They took off their shoes and started toward the waves.

As they stepped barefoot in the sand they saw other things — a plastic cigarette lighter, a piece of styrofoam, a can, a bottle, a sack from a fast-food restaurant. Their steps slowed and their smiles disappeared as they continued toward the water.

As the waves came in, tugging on their legs, they stood looking out to the sea disappearing into the sky. As they turned back toward the beach, they both heard a sigh and looked at each other.

"**W**as that you?" he asked her.

"Well, maybe I did sigh," she replied, "but I thought maybe it was you. It was so big."

"Let's walk until sunset," he suggested. She smiled in agreement. As they walked, they met older people and younger people. Some smiled and said, "Hello." They smiled and returned the greeting. Once they stopped and had a great time helping three children build a sand sculpture. As they worked together, they pushed aside a piece of jagged orange plastic and a piece of metal from a car.

For a moment no one said anything as the waves crashed on the shore. The man and woman looked at each other and at the children. The children were looking at them and then they all heard the sigh. It was so big, the sound of the sea disappeared and they couldn't see anything but each other, their hands in the sand and the garbage around the sculpture.

16

Suddenly a call came. It was from the children's parents. "Time to go now." They all looked into each other's faces and at the sculpture. The children jumped up. The oldest boy stopped for a moment before leaving and said, "I hope you will come back another day."

"We will," the man and woman responded together. "We will come back tomorrow." As the children walked away with their parents, the man and woman added seaweed to the sculpture, then rose from their knees and looked out into space. Clouds had turned pink and there, in the pale blue between, was a silvery crescent of light, the new moon. Before they got back to their cottage, darkness came to the beach and stars sparkled in the deep blue of space. There was no one else on the beach then as they walked. The sigh was gone, but they remembered it. They remembered the big sigh as they turned on the lights in their cottage, as they had dinner and when they turned off the lights and went to bed. Soon the sound of the tide made them forget and they fell asleep.

T he next morning the man and woman rose early and went out. It was different then the day before. They couldn't see anything but dim outlines in the mist. The air felt wet like in the bathroom after a hot shower, but it felt cool also. The mist was close and it was a little scary, the kind of scary that makes you want more, that makes you want to see what's next. They felt excited. As they descended the bank to the beach, they couldn't see much beyond each other. They looked down and there at their feet, the garbage loomed large. Then the sigh returned. It was so big in the mist, their excitement was gone and they turned back. While they made breakfast, they talked about the beauty of the sea and the beach; about the children, the misty morning and about the sigh.

"We must do something about this," they said. After breakfast they gathered all the bags they had and went out, down the bank onto the beach. The mist was not as thick now and some others were out walking as gulls flew, landed and took off. They each opened a bag and started picking up all that did not belong there. As they worked, the three children with whom they had sculpted were suddenly there.

"Can we help you?" The oldest boy asked. Soon they each had a bag and without any instructions, they knew what to do. Before long an older couple saw what was happening, people who had been saddened by the sigh. After watching for a moment, they left and came back with bags and picked up garbage. Then there was another and another and another who joined in.

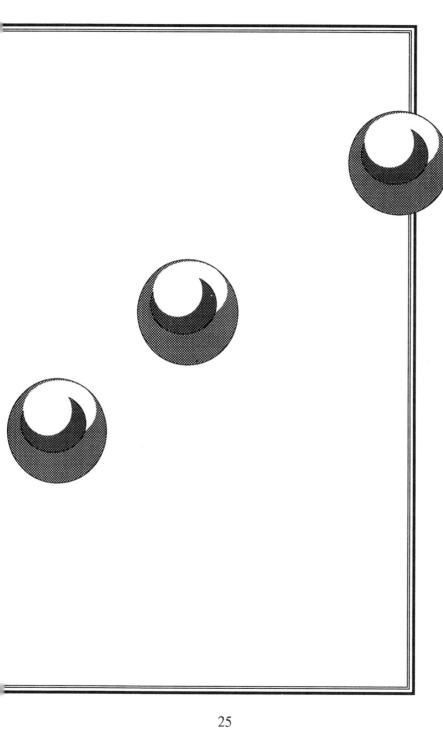

By mid-day, the mist was gone and the beach was different than the day before. Shells glittered in the sunlight near shiny seaweed on the sand. Kites were flying in the breeze. Gulls flew on angular wings and waves crashed on the sparkling sand. Older people walked, their faces warm and happy with smiles. Younger people walked and ran and laughed joyously. Children played together and terns ran in the tide, dipping their long beaks in for something to eat. All on the beach belonged there, fit together like long ago.

I was a new day and the sigh was gone.